Andy's Dandy Day

A Day With Nothing To Do

A Story Written and Illustrated
By David Medhurst

Andy Rabbit woke up to sunshine.

Andy also woke up to a whole day to do whatever he wanted to do! First thing Andy wanted to do was have breakfast. That part was easy to figure out because Andy's tummy told him so with a loud rumble. As Andy was getting himself ready he kept thinking about what he would do with this sunny day.

Downstairs went Andy to find his mommy in the kitchen just putting his breakfast on the table.

"Good morning," said his mommy with a big smile. "I heard you coming, so I got your breakfast for you!"

"Thank you mommy," said Andy as he sat at the table to enjoy his favourite breakfast.

"So," said his mommy, "what are your plans for today?"

"I don't know yet" said Andy.

His mother smiled "I'm sure you will think of something."

After breakfast, Andy stepped into the front yard. It seemed like such a shame that on such a nice day he had nothing to do.

He looked glumly down at the ground and scuffed his feet around.

Well," he thought to himself, "maybe I will follow the path and see if I can find something to do."

As Andy started off his mood lightened. After all, it was still a beautiful day and the breeze felt nice on his face. So nice, in fact, that he decided to run. Running made the breeze even stronger, and that made him feel even happier.

"Weeeeee" laughed Andy as he stretched out his arms to pretend he was a bird flying through the air. Around in circles and up the path he flew until he rounded a corner and met Mr. Moose.

Mr. Moose was the oldest of everyone that he knew and he was surely the biggest.

"Hello Mr. Moose," said Andy as he looked up to where his neighbour towered above him.

"Hello Andy," smiled old Mr. Moose. "Heard you coming a ways off.
What are you up to on this fine morning?"

"Well," said Andy, "I was looking for something to do, and while I was doing that
I was flying like a bird …. Or at least pretending to."

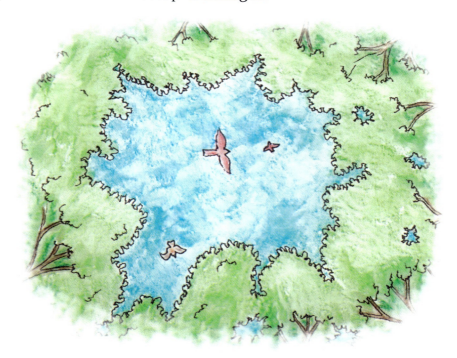

"Something to do?" questioned Mr. Moose as he smiled down at Andy and then slowly
looked off into the woods. "Listen to the trees Andy. They will almost always tell you
what to do."

"Really?" asked Andy as he tilted his head in order to hear better.

"Yes," whispered Mr. Moose knowingly. "For instance, do you hear the way the leaves are rustling gently? If they were making a lot more noise, I would say they were telling you to get your kite! Now, if you heard the leaves rattling and flying past you, then they would be telling you to get your warm coat because winter is coming".

Andy listened very hard but couldn't tell what the trees were saying. "What do you think they are saying now?" asked Andy.

"I would say that on such a beautiful day, they are telling you to enjoy yourself," said Mr. Moose as he scooched way down and ruffled Andy's head.

"Well thanks, Mr. Moose, that's exactly what I will try to do."

"And so will I," said the elder Moose as he lifted his face into the sunlight, closed his eyes, and smiled.

Andy started back along the path again with thoughts of the trees talking to him. He would have to pay more attention from now on.

The path gently wound its way down as the trees slowly thinned out and Andy found himself by the river.

Standing by the shore overlooking a collection of logs and sticks was Mr. Beaver. Now Mr. Beaver was quite a portly fellow and very careful about his appearance.

"Must always look one's best," Mr. Beaver would say. "After all, if you look nice and snappy, you make others happy!" which Mr. Beaver always followed with a chortle and a thump from his walking stick, which by the way, he had made himself and was quite fond of.

"Hello Mr. Beaver!" called Andy as he approached the shore.

"Why, hello Andy!" Mr. Beaver answered back. "What brings a fine fellow, such as yourself, all the way down here so early in the day?" But before Andy could answer, Mr. Beaver continued on. "And well dressed too! You look like you have a plan, all put together, and know exactly how you are going to go about it."

"Well, not exactly" said Andy. "I thought I would go for a walk while I tried to figure out what to do."

"A good plan makes for a good day!" exclaimed Mr. Beaver, "As a matter of fact, I was just here making one myself, and now that I am looking at you, and those wonderful ears of yours, my plan just came together, and for that, I thank you!"

Andy tilted his head with a puzzled look. "My ears?"

Mr. Beaver stood up straight and with another chortle, thumped the ground with his walking stick.

"Let me explain Andy." He turned and pointed to one of the old fallen trees lying on the ground. "Now, take a look at this log. See the way it goes up, nice and straight, all the way up to the top? That log is good for many things, if you are needing a straight log. With that log, I can make a nice straight line, right across the top of the dam over there.

"Now that other log over there, has a nice 'Y' shape, which I immediately remembered, when I looked at your ears! With that 'Y', I can put up another log and have it held in place. Yup, that will do the trick! Now my plan has all come together!"

Mr. Beaver turned back towards Andy and gave him a thorough inspection. "Let me look you over once more son. Yup, you look nice and snappy, and ready for whatever you plan to do today, and I can tell you, whether you planned it or not, you've already put a smile on my face. I have to get back to work now, so give my best to your family, and make sure you plan to have a good day son."

"Thank you Mr. Beaver," said Andy with a matching smile as he headed off again. Andy was feeling pretty good, even though he still hadn't figured out what to do.

The path wound up and around the river and through some trees until it came to a clearing at the top of the hill. Sitting in the sunshine next to his hole was Mr. Gopher, quietly munching on a handful of clover.

"Hello Mr. Gopher!" said Andy.

Mr. Gopher looked over his shoulder and smiled at Andy.
"Hello Andy. Would you like some clover?" asked Mr. Gopher.

"Oh, no thank you, I already had my breakfast," answered Andy politely.

"Breakfast?" questioned Mr. Gopher. "It's getting on towards lunch time now! You must be having a busy day to lose track of time like that."

"Not really," said Andy. "I actually haven't even decided what I am going to do today."

Mr. Gopher smiled at Andy. "Come have a seat for a minute, and if you change your mind about the clover, just reach down and grab a handful. It tastes especially nice in the sunshine."

Andy looked down at the clover. It did look good and he did feel a little hungry after walking. Besides, he would need some energy if he was to figure out what he was going to do today. "Well, if you are sure it's alright," said Andy.

"Go right ahead young man," said Mr. Gopher, and the two sat in the late morning sun, enjoying the breeze and pointing out all the beautiful things they could see in the valley below them.

After a time, Andy stood and brushed off his pants. "I must be going Mr. Gopher. Thank you for the clover. I really enjoyed our visit."

"So did I, Andy," replied Mr. Gopher. "Drop by any time."

So with a smile and a wave Andy was on his way.

Skipping down the path, Andy realized that half the day was gone and he still hadn't figured out what he was going to do. Andy rounded another corner and was greeted by a sight of extreme activity.

Moving quickly from one spot to another was Mr. Squirrel. Mr. Squirrel would stop, look around, and then swiftly move over to another spot where he would gather into his arms the acorns that lay scattered about the clearing. Sometimes upon inspection an acorn would not be up to standard and Mr. Squirrel would leave it behind.

When he had all he could hold, Mr. Squirrel quickly raced up his tree and handed them over to Mrs. Squirrel. Andy continued to watch as Mr. Squirrel hurried back down the tree and again started scurrying around the clearing in a bent over posture.

After a couple of minutes, Mr. Squirrel's scurrying brought him right next to Andy. Suddenly stopping, he looked up from the ground, spotting Andy for the first time.

Placing his hands in the small of his back Mr. Squirrel straightened up with a satisfying crackle.

"Oh hello Andy! Didn't see you there! No sir, didn't see you for one second until I almost collected you as a nut," Mr. Squirrel said with a friendly smile and a chattery chuckle.

"Hello Mr. Squirrel," Andy said.
"You look awfully busy."

"Busy?" responded Mr. Squirrel. "Why, yes yes! Busy indeed! Have to get things ready! Have to be prepared! You need to be prepared Andy, not just for today but next week and next month! Why, the work I am doing today is for next Tuesday. Yes sir I am way ahead of the game."

"Here, have a nut," said Mr. Squirrel as he handed Andy an acorn.
"What about yourself, Andy? What are you busy doing today?"

"Actually," said Andy, "I still haven't quite figured out what I am doing today."

Mr. Squirrel paused and stretched again as he looked at Andy with surprise.
"You best be getting on with things, Andy. It will soon be tomorrow before you figure out what you're doing today."

And with that he bent down and picked up a load of nuts and scurried off into the woods, leaving Andy with a puzzled look on his face.

Andy hopped along finishing his nut when he came to an open sunny glade full of flowers, with butterflies and bees busily droning back and forth. In the middle of all the sunshine stood Mr. Bear, intently watching the bees as he hopped from foot to foot and gently clapped his great big paws.

"Hello Mr. Bear!" called Andy. He really liked Mr. Bear. He wasn't as tall as Mr. Moose but he sure was bigger than anyone else Andy knew. Plus, he always had honey.

"Hello Andy!" exclaimed Mr. Bear, and with two big bounds he was right beside Andy. Reaching down he gave Andy's head a soft ruffle with his enormous paw. "How nice to see you on such a sunny afternoon! What brings you into this neck of the woods? Come for some honey maybe? As for me, I would travel a long ways for honey," said Mr. Bear while he licked his lips at the thought of his favourite food.

"Not actually" said Andy, although the thought of honey did sound yummy even after all the clover at Mr. Gopher's house and the nice nut Mr. Squirrel gave him. "I just ended up here because this is where the path took me. I was out looking for something to do."

Mr. Bear smiled down at Andy and gave his head another gentle pat. "Well now Andy, I myself don't really have to think about that too much because I keep things pretty simple. I just enjoy the day for what it is."

"Really?" asked Andy.
"How do you do that?"

"Bees!" exclaimed Mr. Bear.
"Bees and honey! I take care of
the bees, and they take care of me.
That's all. That and a good scratch!
That's what days are all about!" he
said with laugh. "Well, at least if you're
me, and that's because I don't need very
much. You give me my bees to tend to
when the sun is warm and my cozy
den when winter has its way with the
world and I'm content." Mr. Bear
paused, then chuckled. "Oh oh,
I guess my den is one more thing!"

"That sounds pretty nice Mr. Bear," said Andy.

"Pretty nice for me, Andy" said Mr. Bear, "but it's not for everyone. I would say at your age, you have time to figure out what's nice for you." Mr. Bear looked at Andy with a smile and patted his tummy. "Until then, how about a little honey to see if you might be a bear kind of bunny?"

Andy giggled at the thought of himself as a bear. "Maybe just a little, please and thanks."

"Be right back," said Mr. Bear, and with two big bounds he was over at a nearby tree.

Gently brushing aside the bees, he reached into a hole in the tree trunk and with two more big bounds, was back at Andy's side with two dripping pieces of honeycomb, a small Andy sized one and a much bigger Mr. Bear sized piece.

Together they stood in the sunshine and pointed out the different types of flowers and butterflies that covered the meadow. Once all the honey was finished, Andy licked his paws and with a big sticky smile, thanked Mr. Bear once again.

"You are most welcome," said Mr. Bear with an equally sticky smile. "I guess you should be on your way so your Mom doesn't worry. Besides, I should get back to my bees, and maybe a little more honey." Mr. Bear looked down at Andy and winked.

Andy giggled, and with a wave started back along the path. Mr. Bear was right. It was getting late and he had been out all day.

Andy quickly hopped along the path, sometimes trying to scurry like Mr. Squirrel or bound like Mr. Bear.

Eventually the path led him back to his own house where his mother was standing out front. "I was just coming out to look for you," said his mother with a smile. "My, you have been gone all day. I hope you stopped for lunch."

"Oh, yes Mommy. I actually had lunch with Mr. Gopher and then later I had a snack with Mr. Squirrel."

"Mr. Gopher and Mr. Squirrel!" exclaimed Andy's mother, "That's a little ways off. How did you end up over there?"

"Well," started Andy, "I walked along the forest path. It was such a nice day that next thing I knew I met Mr. Moose. He told me how to listen to the trees. I didn't know they had so much to say!"

"My!" said Andy's mother. "Mr. Moose too! But what about Mr. Squirrel and Mr. Gopher?"

"Oh," said Andy "Well, when I left Mr. Moose, I kept following the path that took me down by the river where Mr. Beaver was, and I helped him plan out his dam."

"Mr. Beaver?" Andy's mother said. "You didn't mention him."

"Oh yes, the path goes right down by the riverbank and that's where Mr. Beaver's dam is," responded Andy.

"I see," said Andy's mother. "But, when did you meet Mr. Gopher?"

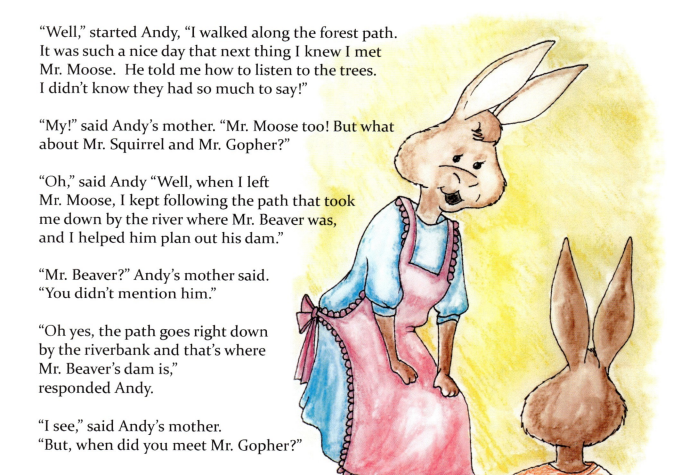

"Well," continued Andy, "when I left Mr. Beaver, I followed the trail up the hill to the top of the meadow. It's so beautiful there, and Mr. Gopher was sitting by his house enjoying the sun, and the clover is so fresh, and Mr. Gopher offered me some, so we sat and had lunch together. You should see Mommy. You can see the whole valley from up there. I could see Mr. Beaver's dam and the river all the way through."

"Yes," said his mother, "that does sound very nice, and I am glad you had something to eat. So what happened next?"

"I stayed with Mr. Gopher for quite a while because it was so nice in the sun, but then I figured I better start heading home because I was quite a ways away. That was when I met Mr. Squirrel."

"I see," his mother encouraged with a smile. "And how was Mr. Squirrel?"

"Busy!" exclaimed Andy. "I've never seen someone move around so much and boy, can he ever climb trees! He is really nice and he gave me a nut."

"Not too close to dinner I hope," interrupted his mother.

"No no, Mommy," assured Andy. "And besides, I'm really hungry from all my walking today. Even the honey Mr. Bear gave me hasn't spoiled my appetite."

"Mr. Bear!" laughed his mother. "When did you meet him?"

"He was out in the meadow with the bees while I was on my way home," explained Andy. "Mr. Bear is the biggest and most gentle of everybody I know," Andy said fondly.

"And he has honey," said his mother with a smile. "Well Andy, did you ever figure out what you were going to do today?" His mother looked at him with love and that special knowing mothers have, as if she already knew the answer to her question.

"No." said Andy as they went inside. "And I think it was the best day of nothing to do I ever had."

The End

For Rosa who believes in my dreams and loves me for who I am
and for Christopher who is my inspiration in all things.

93163881R00020

Made in the USA
Columbia, SC
11 April 2018